This MAMMOTH belongs to

_____ ___

_____

_____

WHAT ON EARTH...?

WHAT ON EARTH...?

By Hazel Townson
Illustrated by Mary Rees

MAMMOTH

First published in Great Britain 1991 by Andersen Press Ltd
Published 1994 by Mammoth
an imprint of Reed Consumer Books Ltd
Michelin House, 81 Fulham Road, London SW3 6RB
and Auckland, Melbourne, Singapore and Toronto
Text copyright © Hazel Townson 1991
Illustrations copyright © Mary Rees 1991

ISBN 0 7497 1213 9

A CIP catalogue record for this title
is available from the British Library

Produced by Mandarin Offset
Printed and bound in Hong Kong

"You go ahead and have a nice bath, dear," said Dad. "I'll keep an eye
on Laura."

"Laura! What on earth do you think you're doing under the table?"

"Why on earth are you bouncing up and down on your mother's favourite chair?"

"What on earth do you think you're doing to the cat?"

"What on earth do you think you're doing with the garden hose?"

"What on earth do you think you're doing on the doormat?"

"Why on earth are you wearing your mother's winter coat?"

"What on earth do you think you're doing with my umbrella?"

"Where on earth do you think you're going with Grandpa's deck-chair?"

"What on earth do you think you're doing with your sister's make-up?"

"What on earth are you doing climbing up the wall?"

Just then Mum returned, "What have you two been doing? And…

where on earth is Laura?"